W0259518

IN THE LIGHTS OF A MIDNIGHT PLOW

IN THE LIGHTS OF A MIDNIGHT PLOW

David Hickey

BIBLIOASIS

FIRST EDITION

Library and Archives Canada Cataloguing in Publication

Hickey, David, 1977–
In the lights of a midnight plow / David Hickey.

Poems.
1-897231-09-01

1. Title.

PS8615.I3415 2006 C811'.6 C2006-902472-3

Edited by
Eric Ormsby

Typesetting & Design:
Karen Veryle Monck

We acknowledge the support of the Canada Council for the Arts for our publishing program.

PRINTED AND BOUND IN CANADA

For my parents

Contents

The Disappeared Forest

A Hole in the Sea

The Afterlives of Ted Williams

The Streetlights' Stationary Tribe

The Glass Desert

. . . my memory takes over out here so I walk through two worlds,
haunting the place I grew up and being haunted by it,
a ghost without allegiance in houses possessed by the living.

– Shane Rhodes "Home Roads"

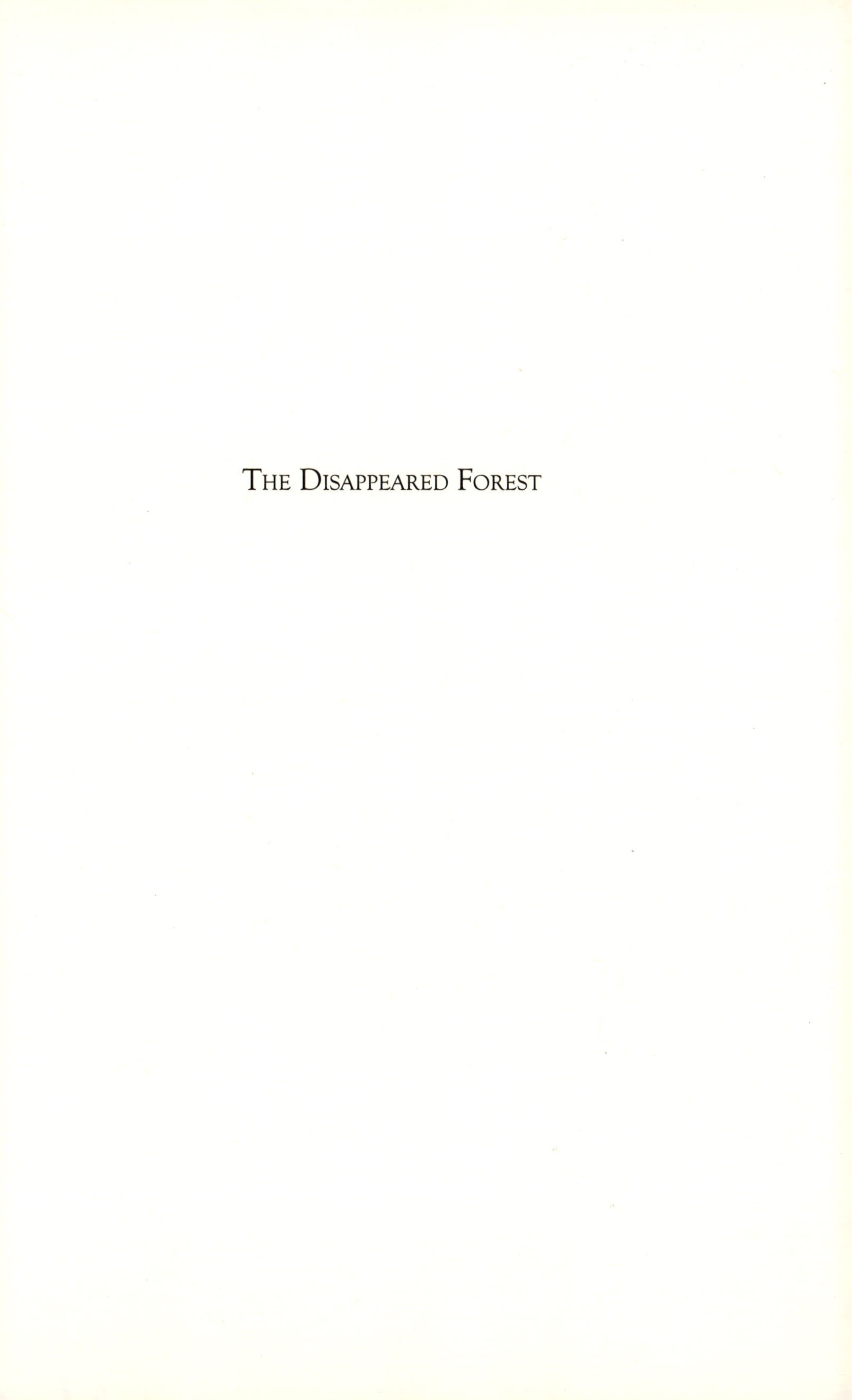

The Disappeared Forest

Space Between Fires

Always that space,
the uncut fields

where the light
between bonfires

fails to reach:
where you wander

home at night,
thinking your lost

baseball might lie
underfoot; thinking,

I saw a skunk here
once and Jesus

that brush of white
better not be

what I think it is;
thinking the ocean lies

miles away but
feels like it's grabbing

hold of your back
pocket, a hold of some

part of your past
that's catching

up with you, running
out of breath,

waving a light
in the darkness.

Harvest

She was picking black-eyed Susies. I know because those dark
suns were burning dry in her hand. Not that it would
happen now, a tractor would scare us off a dozen acres before

it reached us, but a horse drawn blade has a way with
a pasture, and it came like a breeze to her ankle. My God,
the blood there was. We stuck her leg in a basin, what she had

to fill it with like rain tipping a barrow. Sure, she got rushed
to town, spent the next three weeks in hospital, maybe
that's why she's a nurse now, who knows. All I remember is

how she kept filling that basin. And how afterwards,
mom just told us to go finish what the morning
hadn't seen done while she hung our clothes to the field.

The Hanging Tree

Gave the field a centre to rush towards

a centripetal scarecrow
hung with swings and sparrows that circled
as though decorating
fairground air

underneath it
every thing pushed up

snow field mice
short grass the colour of filthy pennies

every morning
we lined up at the bus stop and watched
as it took attendance

we studied its branches
wanting proof
someone once hung there
like an electrified kite

but day after day
it disappointed us

it just pinned the field
with a half-dozen roots
and pulled itself
deeper in earth.

Strawberries

My cousin threw them six rows over,
pulling up the dirt like a catcher
with a runner asleep in the field. No farmer
or crow passing by could tell, but
those tosses bloomed to bruises later,
so I spent the summer crouched in leaf.
My naked palms full, I raked up
the bottom of the plant, careful to judge
the fruit in my hand: the too early
white, the dark begging for harvest, I was
learning to pick or let blossom.
But if I drifted a moment too long in blue
above, hoping for rain to send us
home, no one seemed to mind. And when
my hands went back behind
my head, and I felt the cool signal of soil,
I never knew how long I slept
or why no one bothered to wake me.

Barns

Starlight especially seems to love them . . .
– Tim Bowling

He wants you to believe it's more
than a slope with a timber garden,
a rise in the field where disheveled
planks break over stacks of grain.

He wants you to believe his barns are
the starlit descendants of Bethlehem,
not the last trees of a disappeared forest,
all gossamer and ghost bark, smelling

of horse hair and bull seed, flesh and
digested grass, the inside panels rotten
with life. And he'd rather a barn grow
out of the ground & shift in darkness,

flawless except for the hole in
the roof requiring a hand anchored
by hammer and moonlight, insisting
an old farmer lean against a frosted
plank, shingling the stars in place.

Airways

Boys have bird-souls.
– Don McKay

Which might explain why
we perched there, shirts off

in summer, looking
out at the miles-away river,

the hay loft doors swung
wide to nowhere but

down. Why we felt the need to
leap from such heights,

casting ourselves to poorly
stacked bails spread

in the yard below. Why
it was a brief flight, a denial

of parachutes, a c'mon
to the crows. Why

the fall sometimes knocked
the wind out of you,

woke some small bird
perched between your ribs,

swallowing and
coughing up stone.

Country Landscaping

At best, it's an awkward proposition,
this convincing stones to rustle.
All the broken soil you can spread
and still the lot comes up
beech tree, sparse green, thistle,
leaves you with a taste of old apricots
and lemons, especially when
the wind lifts half the seed before
the rest takes, the rain never
falling when it's supposed to,
it's like a wound unwilling to heal.

You can rake it all day, pull up
rocks and roots of trees
long since forgotten by hawks, cross it all
a thousand times with the wood
of a thick-tooth rake, but
it's still half-yard, half-reluctance,
as if the nearby sea had some
say in the foreground, all that salt
forming a dry breeze
for the sake of a rusted contrast.

Sure, once I saw a lot get worked
over for days. The whole thing
hauled and planted so the hut of a cottage
could stand out in a company
of pine. All those hours
and the damn lawn never grew,
the company shrugged off
in a shitbox truck, and the owner,
not sure whether to curse
seed or soil, stood under the arc
of a wind-stiffened gull,
kicking at the ground beneath it.

Cape Bear, Prince Edward Island, 1941

I am going to see the U-boats hovering
one-half mile in the Strait.

I am bringing sandwiches, a homemade
hand-grenade I made from a broken
rake and kerosene from my father's lantern.

If there are cows at Cape Bear I will steal
their bells so no one will hear me coming.

I will pull strands of wool from my sweater
and weave them with lengths of grass.

I will crouch, imitating the field's posture.

When the sun
disappears off Cape Bear I will slide
driftwood into the ocean until
I know the tide's direction,

and when the tide is low, and the moon full
enough to walk by, I will stroll
into the water with a grenade above my head.

Decorated with waves, I will float with
the weight of stars on my stomach
and the sway of the earth beneath me.

The first human periscope, I will
spy on the cows at pasture.

I will be seen drifting days from now,
armed and looking at shore.

Preservation

These boys will never outgrow their jean jackets,
this photograph, the cliffs and the tattered maps

the wind wears into them. They will not lose
their way among the shoreline's rocky bruises,

or forget where the best spots are to hide
from the heat of an afternoon sun. It's the tide,

this boy, and the way he points at a wave
that will preserve them, the hand and how

it staves their leaving: they're looking down,
perhaps at some broken piece of driftwood

crowned with rotting seaweed, some bundle swept
from the camera's flash. None of them expect

to be preserved this carefully, their hands
in their pockets, or pulling up strands of grass.

The Field's Afterthoughts

Behind my brother's home, a field in October. The harvester
has crawled over,
the crop pulled and gathered in the spiral turnover of fall.
Somewhere

past the tree line, the cows are calling across the earth, and
only a few strides
from where the yard has ceased to grow, three boys travel
back and forth

for the potatoes left by a farmer who won't mind their filling
shirts with them.
They'll be out for hours, pulling the weeds from spring,
examining the field's

afterthoughts left out to sore in the sun: they'll search under
diced leaves,
white root, filling clear bags with shapes that will sprig in my
brother's garage,

such offerings alive as they are, seasonal as the boys
who appear on the step, covered in field and selling their
goods at the door.

Amusement Park Dragons

A mechanic polishes
a season's worth of sweaty

prints, each smudge of warm
evening air giving up

its leathery grip as the moon
punches its own pass

through the dusk, riding
high above a circus of lights.

Before he locks up,
the mechanic will tug them

towards a plywood
cave, and the dragons, wheels

sparking along the pavement,
will huff out the last

bit of summer before settling
their wings to rust.

A Fresh Shirt

A rag caught fire and the garage blew clear out.
You can imagine the mess of me, all blistered
and soft, like liquid running for the drain.

Couldn't very well go to the hospital without
a clean shirt so I went to your Aunt Fran's
instead, and when I got there she said

what happened? and I said the garage blew
and she said, look, your shirt's halfway
into your back. So I looked in the mirror and

she was right, I was half-gone, blue
with strands of dark cotton stuck inside me,
like I was a welder's torch and my skin

the constant flame. That red in her face
as she went to her father's closet and pulled
out a fresh one for me, all pressed and

full of static, those sparks and the bits of metal
in my back as I headed out the door.

Night Shift

The evening before the night shift he stays
up late to drain the days from his body.

Tomorrow a thousand sheets of cardboard
will lift by, each a slow, seagull flight,

their corrugated wings floating to the end
of the line where they divide the shift into piles,

slip off in trucks to Michigan. It's a hard cut,
he says, going from days to nights,

the body stretches out like a field losing
its sun, a landscape tired of its own, sad twilight.

A hard cut, he says, a thousand
cardboard birds in brief nocturnal flight.

Evening at the Charlottetown Airport

Hands spaded in the earth, my grandfather
watches another plane bring its wheels
to his farm. He can't pull free of the soil

so he holds tight to a column of field, overripe
bulbs of runway burning red under
wings in the evening. For all he's grown

he doesn't remember planting such colour,
the dusk-lit rows showing pilots where
they can and cannot land. When the plane taxis

along the runway, my grandfather kneels
next to the airstrip glowing.
He buries the day's sun in the ground.

Landscape, Looking Back

This Island suffers from a gentility of
low hills that discourage reaching up . . .
– John Mackenzie
"landscape, from lowdown"

Suffers the lot of us, hell-bent
on turning up the fields,
marrying ourselves to the discernible
effect a corroding star
insists on a torn pocket of earth:

suffers the study of soil
mechanics, suffers the poison
of folk, suffers the hard
turning gears and bolts of cliffs
wearing away at the edge:

suffers the recitation of dunes,
the hemming of fields, the unnecessary
charting of tides (south
shore moons, moonshine tides)
and shaped as it is,

suffers the fate of frequent
return, suffers those who vacation
half-out with the tide,
lamenting some sky-born song
only the gulls can hear.

Another List of Things Left Behind

Horses in the yard, the clothes line
and the dangle of towels

blowing to a cluster of trees
downwind. The dented mailbox

stuck to a ditch like something forgotten
on trash day, the stretched-out

fields of thistle, the house blood red
in winter, and sometimes

the ocean, tightening
with the break of a late fall tide.

Blessing

May skunks piss on you nightly
        and may the full moon cast a warm light on
the fizzle.

        May the organs once held by the parchment of skin
dry to a grave robber's cough.

        May your grandchildren suffer the incurable
disease of relation,

        may your afterlife be spent in a poorly-
built coffin,

        and may all your sins pass through you like
small hungry mouths.

Claims

I have been leaving for months now, letting myself be taken
out by the waves,
back to where the beach bruises with the last carcasses
of summer.

A thousand other summers have lined up before me
to lay their claim
but the sun has burned their flesh and buried them
under its call. I have sat here

since the beginning and listened to the slow rattle of a gull,
its ribcage
a salt-white opening, have kicked at the kelp's tangle,
the dry break of matter

fossilizing the sea. I have torn vegetation, broken the stems
as bones, emptied
a crab shell and thrown the mineral as seed, but found
the ocean

still too much a nod of blue sailing on the planet's back
to care who or what
I blame. Not much in the turn of dunes suggests a path
away from here,

one lit by the first moon seen through snow, cracked
and white as a seashell
found past October, frozen and packed in thyme.
But nothing in the rise

of stars keeps the body from staying awhile longer
under the sky's terrace,
calculating the distance one might travel with so much left
to claim.

A Hole in the Sea

Bypass

Left to its own designs, the heart might choose
to pump water instead, might dig into a plain
of earth until it struck an underground stream,
cause that cold drink to surface, then crawl

back into some sleeping chest. Take this one:
its ribs warmed under the steam of the electric
scalpel while the surgeon's hand worked to seal
the body against its own flooding, then closed

the cavern, the heart like a sunless fruit,
a fistful of leaves pulled from a damp garden.
The scar as a gill, a thin schism closing over
time, proof of some other life, perhaps at sea.

Learning the Butterfly

The arms draw a keyhole, a door through which
an ancient swimmer might cross a darkened
sea. This movement a symphony before

the instruments were invented. The first song was,
of course, water cooling rock, and not long
after, as hills grew on land, among those living

in oceans, a preoccupation with flight.
Maybe the waves became too warm,
so they traded the dictates of celestial currents

for those of air, giving birth to a species that would
negotiate ideas of gravity: their arms
never quite becoming wings, except for a select few

who flew off like colourful pieces
of cloth, dusting hidden mosses as they went.

The 17th-Century Cartographer's Nightmare

Sometimes the map
shifts on its own

and a new land appears
in place of a crafted

sea. Sometimes
an ink well contains

the Atlantic ocean,
and a single mis-stroke

fills colonies
with water, orchards

of coral and tide.
And sometimes,

even awake, a candle
spills on the table,

its flame sets sail
across the darkening

map, devouring
the anonymous green.

Channel Markers

Never float up from underwater shipyards
        where lost deckhands are

hammering a new sky; are neither copper islands
        or rusted moons, the muted

bells of flooded monasteries, Christmas ornaments
        or fallen space

capsules, pteragon shells or petrified mammals
        tied by chain.

They offer little more than highway
        signs, a tip and nod to passing boats:

a starboard red, an outgoing
        green, their bodies the aftermath of gulls.

Once, though, like a cork lost in a milk bottle,
        I stood at the bottom of one,

the marker sawed in half and planted in a backyard
        garden, cleaning the metal sides

while goldfish woke around my ankles.
        I watched as each one arrived from hibernation;

a dozen orange leaves
        blown clear of the spring snow,

they travelled back and forth
        as though they had not spent winter

along the marker's bottom, but were emerging
        from another body

of water, swimming up now through
        the open buoy, which felt like a hole in the sea.

A Letter to the Corinthians

I took you for camelled desert
walkers, spreading gospel
like the rumour of a Galilean
storm. I believed the letters

a response to the woman
I dreamed of, the ruined sheets
spread across my bible
like an unbroken sea, proof

you measured me out
in arm-lengths to the nearest
sun. I pulled letters
from the priest's mouth and

held them in clusters,
as handfuls of castaway
stars small enough to fit
in a traveller's pocket.

Your words I took for olives,
your bodies for the dune's
garland, and your parchment
the cold rapture of sand.

Interruptions on a Summer Evening

A moth, the last insect
I would pilot from a dying earth,
the creature Noah mistook
for dust, rests among socks on
the dresser, flying now and
then, holding back sleep
like a night guard manning
a dam. I grab after the body but
it's more dress than wind,
weightless, some fallen
piece of a Yukon moon. I try
again but now the phone is ringing
past the hall, in a lampless
room where I am talking to someone
I haven't heard from
in too long, and we're trading
news like neighbours back
from summer vacation, showing
each other bright postcards
from across the lawn, our voices
hung wide as sheets on
the line, filling up
the air like excited sails of cloth.

The Secret of Disappearing Bodies

We mistook you for Jesus in a dark suit, your eyes
following us through the living rooms of all

our relatives. The uncle none of us knew past
a photograph, the one who would have snuck us

liquor at weddings and wakes, failed to notice
how much we grew but liked the piercing,

the dragon tattoo, the increasing length of our hair.
This is why we believed it was a crow's

nest you climbed towards, decked in a yellow
slicker and armed with the Captain's orders

to chart the first star clear of the storm.
This is why you flew off like a kite, your jacket

loosening in the wind until you were nothing
but a ribbon undulating high above

the sea. Eventually, we learned about the nights
before, how they played out in pool halls,

all that smoke and slate, part of you already
receding like a hand from a table. We heard about

an accident other than your own, and wondered
how glad you were leaving the land behind,

the city and its persistent asking. . . . But then
you walk out of memory down Great George Street,

board that Irving tanker, and disappear off
the bow. Tell us the secret of disappearing bodies.

We're old enough to know what happens to the flesh
years after it's done dying. Tell us how

a man might abandon the ocean and pry
open the mouth of a cloud, how

he might convince a wind with little
more than a well-tied hitch,

then sit with a breeze
in his stomach, the earth a swift craft below.

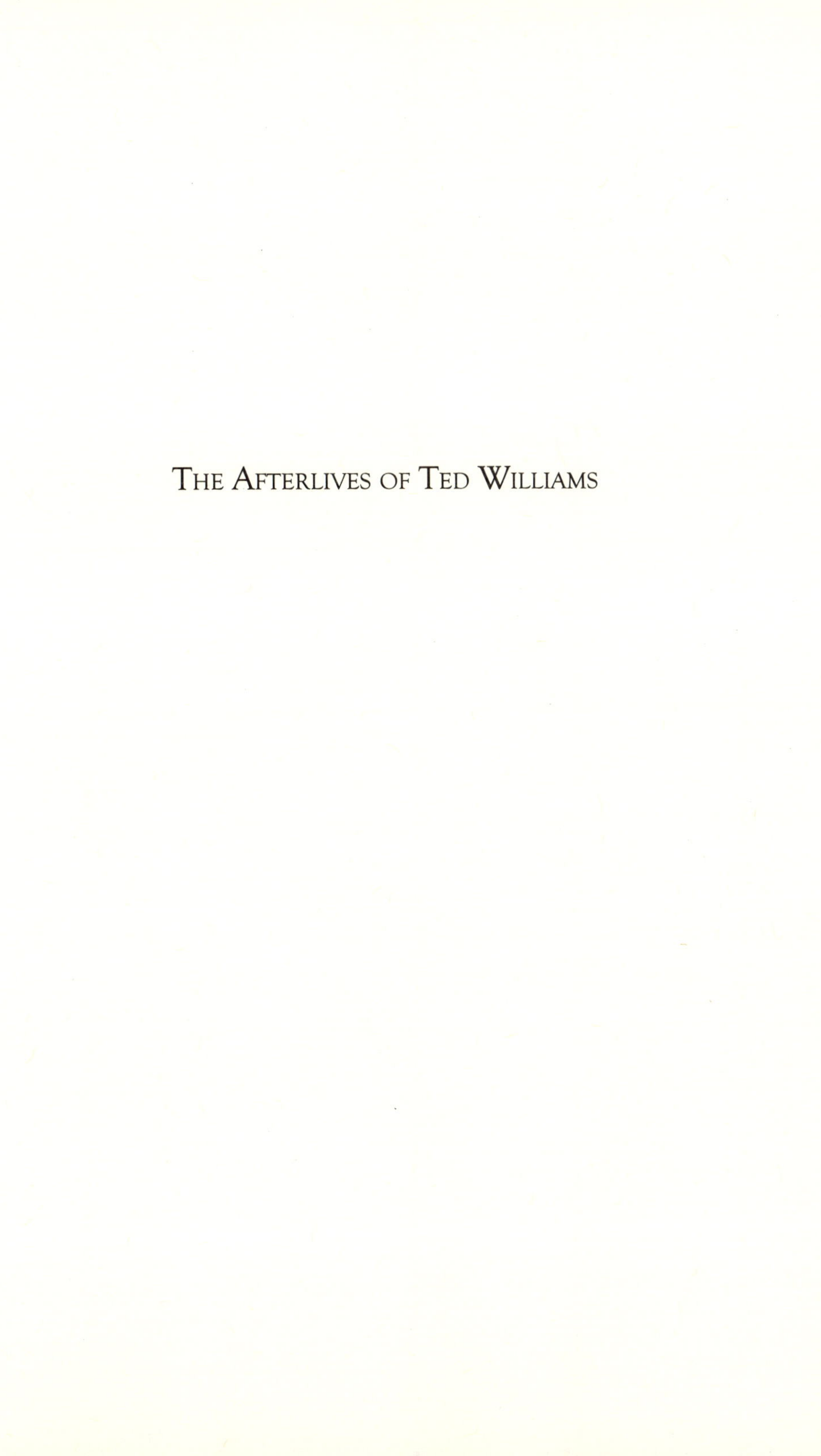

The Afterlives of Ted Williams

Weather Hotline

For $1.49 a minute a woman will talk to you about
storms. She will leave messages about the sun
in other places, a warm front moving near Churchill
Falls, a trough through Frobisher's Bay.

Relentless in her thoughts of rain, careful
with predictions of clearing, she knows
entire gatherings hinge on her arrangement
of the sky, and so she gives

the forecast as though breaking a lover's secret:
each cloud a sordid detail, each snowfall
an infidelity, her voice the loose-shirted someone
who wakes her neighbour's husband

one morning. At work you think of her as ice
breaking eaves, not the snow moving
under your children's feet but the haunted bluster
dogs chase around your home.

You imagine she is shaped
like the jet stream and every bit as measurable.

Northern Appropriation

The Inukshuk has been a northern messenger for thousands of years. Shaped in the likeness of a person, it acts as a guidepost to travellers, to point the way. The Drugstore Pharmacy has chosen to use this symbol, and its simple message to say 'you are not alone.'

– Pamphlet on Erectile Dysfunction

On an icy flat of tundra,
a team of drugstore pharmacists erect
a stolid penis, an arctic satellite
of stone. They invite men
who struggle with impotency to make
the five-day journey across a dozen
northern inlets, a dogsled trek
to the unknown reaches of a snowy land
where early twentieth-century
exhibitions dried in their skin and slowly
coughed up their bones. Under
the soft, unheard decibels
of northern lights, they sit around
quiet campfires, making
an acrid tea from moss at the statue's
base, bringing it to a boil
in generous heaps of snow. By morning,
they are piling stones:
erecting primordial penises in shapes
dating back to their snow
fort dreams. Some men search
for the biggest ones they can
find, stack them widely like fencing
an overgrown garden. Others
for a single flat rock, one they can dry
laundry on, play Friday night
poker and iron their children's clothes.

And still yet others go
in search of the perfect headstone,
the one a traveller will
lean against one thousand years
from now, lost in the middle
of a six-month summer, guessing time
by the sun's steady glow.

The Kidnapping of Lucille Poulin

And He said, if you continue in my word, you shall
know the truth, and the truth shall make you free.
— from the testimony of Lucille Poulin

Wrapping broomsticks with bed sheets,
Lucille's children carry her
off to Neverland. The first morning
she wakes to find her hickory

switch has softened to licorice swirls.
On the second, the lost boys
go fishing with her rosary, place her
wimple atop a crocodile head.

The day after they make Lucille play
patty-cake to the Lord's Prayer,
kiss a lemon tree they claim
as a thousand crosses. On the fourth,

Lucille fails at flight, on the fifth
and sixth she dances for rain.
Then, the seventh day: showing her
a map drawn in the blood

she pulled from their ears, the lines
of latitude carved in their backs,
they send Lucille digging
for the book of God buried among

strands of flax. She digs
to starlight, her hands splintered
with the shovel's wood before
she looks up to find

the children are gone:
they disappeared like fireflies
shifting through fields,
they chased the light as they went.

At the Elementary School Cross Country Meet

The blind boy runs with his teacher in tow,
keeping him close while the rubber soles
of ten-year-olds scuff their way through

the forest. For years he's studied
the darkness, and now it's just
a matter of lifting his feet into flight,

of listening to the other boys go through
the arboretum as he follows the heavy
breathing ahead. He will run the entire way

without knowing the stone waterfall's
timidness, how cleats grind leaves
to a crushed-up red, or when he passes,

how the crowd watches him from fairground
fences, convinced a blind
trapezist must play such tricks on the sky.

The Afterlives of Ted Williams

. . . the son of Ted Williams has shipped the slugger's remains to a company in Phoenix where they will be frozen and his DNA may eventually be sold on the open market, much like the Splendid Splinter's old baseball cards.

– *Globe and Mail* Tuesday, July 9, 2002

Picture them,
seventy-five years from now,
nine old men standing
in a New Brunswick river,
arguing over lures,
keeping their dogs company,
casting line after
line to infinity, pulling up
the descendants of
salmon their father never
caught, each one hung
on the line, scooped up
as if in a baseman's glove.

Picture them on Father's Day,
gathered in a laboratory,
watching him lean like a bat
left in snow, each of them
a strand of DNA more
intricate than a carefully-tied
fly, disliking the way
his eyes look like ice cubes
left at the bottom
of a glass. And then,
at family reunions, flats
of beer cooling

at his feet,
excited Uncles posing
on either side, their wives
clicking away while
small children press sweaty
faces to the chamber,
watch as the snowman

disappears in a fog
of breath, their open mouths
blowing curious 'o's
round as scoreless innings.

Passing Bicycles

Not long after the talking stops near the end
of a three-hour ride, before the flats give
way to hills, the peloton becoming a broken
caterpillar winding for home: when

the side lane disappears and the bicycles
wag through the street, when a chain
slips into the last gear and the sound repeats
like a dozen mouth guards clicking,

then dances down off the line: the pitch
almost as if a boy held a stick
on the side of the road, and for the first
time, the fence went travelling by.

Northern Diamonds

There are children in Labrador
who beg only for July,
for the heat that comes to northern
towns, the dry summer heat
that turns ballparks to graveyards
for snow: children for whom
a basket catch, a sidelong throw,
a double they stretch to a triple
will follow them around
for the afternoon then claim
its space at the table: at dinner
they will be their parents'
small sinuous gods, waving forks
like tridents, claiming
every fly ball as an offering
they stole from the sun. And at night
they will nod off with
the greed of giants, taking sleep
as if it were a base reached
on patience alone, as if the simple
drift of the pitch was
never so easy to judge by.

Herman Johannsen-Smith Visits His Wife's Grave

Look, the snow falls evenly today across
the cemetery, though I think a trail
through the woods still suits you better,
a boulder near a pasture not far
from where I last slept by a stream.
Here, these are the pine cones I gathered
the six miles from St. Sauveur, these
ten years since I cut the track from home.
Tell me, do you think the snow will
hold much longer? It seems no matter
how often I break this trail, the
clouds pass over, and the way back is
not the same. Alice,

most nights I wake
to soreness. I wake as though
I am a ship with a fire in its hull.
I roll on my shoulder, a forest of infidelities
surround me, and you are emerging
from a cove of trees. You knead
my muscles. You work and mend them
over bone until a thin sweat
gathers on my legs. Come closer, I say.
We're old now, yes, but Alice,
at the finish line, when you put those
cold hands on my back....

In the Human Performance Lab

The physiologist hunches over the quadricep
as if it were an immaculate switchboard. Until now,
the man in the chair has been unaware of
the charge his body carries. He thinks, this may explain

the lurking sense my ancestors danced under bolts
of lightening. When the pulse passes through
his muscle, measuring its composition, he forgets
the conduciveness of fibres, and imagines

instead a life spent listening to the air around
power stations, to infinitesimal charges that travel
the length of his spine. He imagines a device
to measure the notes he contains. The sheet music

buried in the muscle. The song the body so
often sings, the progressive scales of its working.

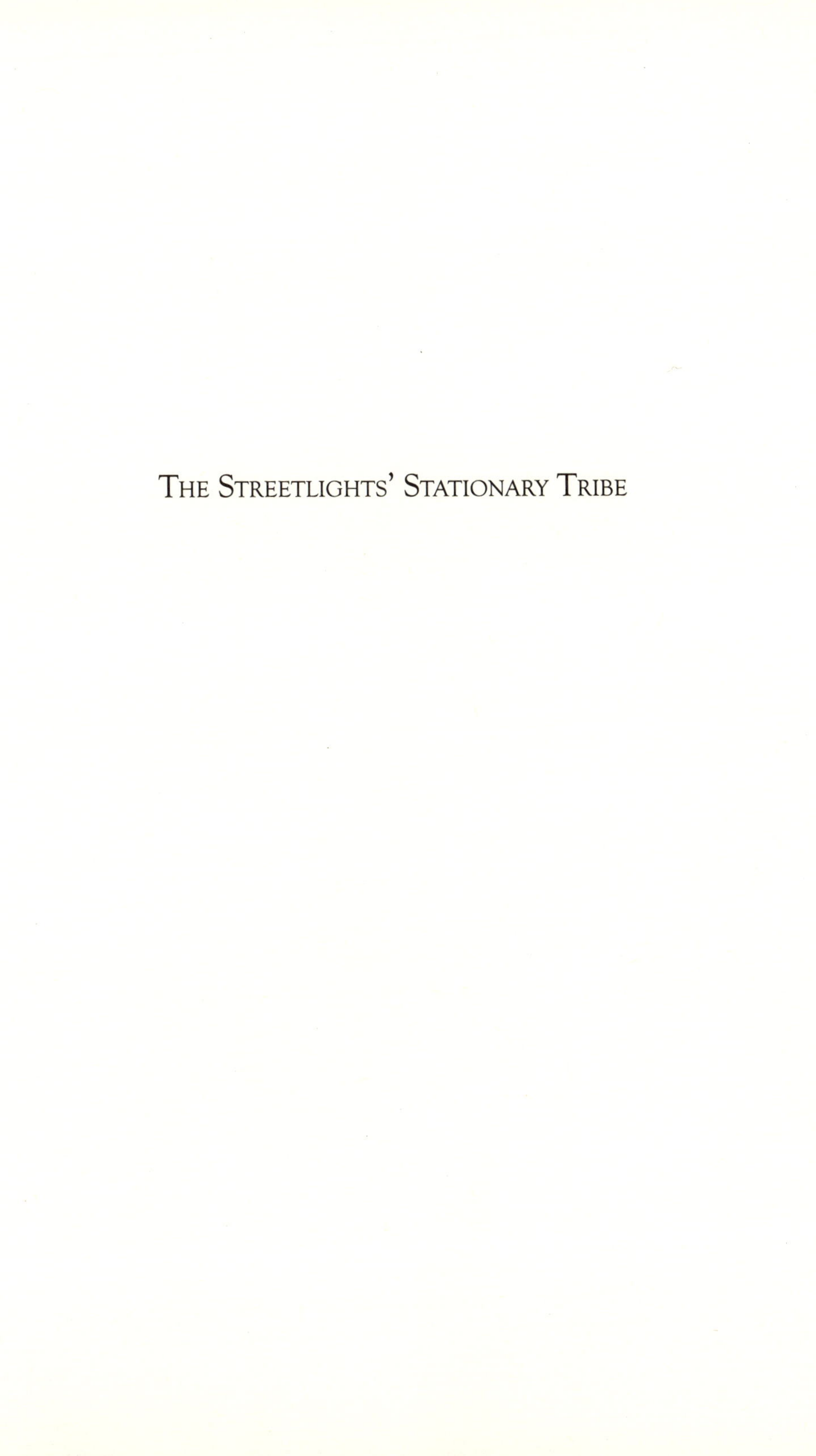

The Streetlights' Stationary Tribe

Evenings

I want two mornings a day.
– Marlene Cookshaw

I want two evenings a day, overlapping
like blankets on a couch, and for it
not to matter which I find myself under,

the stars being more or less the same
when it's time to shovel the walk.

Two evenings to watch salt eat away
at the pavement, the packed snow,
for the dog to warm its head a bit longer

in the dryer's grey fume, for water
to boil on the stove and the kettle's slow

come-on: for steam to fill an empty
house, for kitchen chairs to sit
around the table in silence, and for

the moon, rehearsing itself in the window,
to gather such frost in the dark.

Old Houses

An old house works its way under skin
like a splinter from an unsanded
attic, it gets inside the dogs whose coats

dust the floor, always slightly haunted
by two or three in the morning
when every movement in the kitchen is

a stranger come to steal food from
the pantry, the shelves backlit
by an open fridge. And at times an old

house mistakes mid-afternoon
for evening, and it's hard not to sleep
under the potted peach tree

throwing down its leaves mid-summer,
but then the back stairs
of an old house might be decorated

with Christmas lights in July,
and the reading lamp of an open
room may follow the paneling down

the hall, not far from the back porch
where a toilet sits like part of the family.
Installed not as afterthought but

at the beginning of time, it idles, almost
meditating, the churn of water
raised like a voice through the ceiling.

Note to Self

Paint your room apple green
tomorrow. Do so and frogs will

croak gladly in forests,
your lost sweater will think of you

well, and should friends pass by
in the evening, the day

scattered around them,
floating down

gently on the steady back
of snow, they'll know your window

by the orchard light,
the green tinting the outside

shingles, the walls projecting
the room like a colourful thought

the house once had
down to the street below.

House Fire

Ash for bookends, ashes in the sink,
the baseboards smeared like foreheads
on the first Wednesday of lent. One
hundred years have flown off like a flock

of newspaper ravens and the ink from
their wings has settled across the floor.
Enter every room and you are
the curtains' shadow, the painting burnt

to Impressionism, the shovel left
in the porch since spring. In a bedroom
the letter you sent somewhere near
water and hills–its words have scattered

to rumours of sunlight crossing the second
floor. Having burnt all my books,
deposited the soot in a sleeve, I will send
along a photograph of the hallway's

end: the towels in the closet are fine, but
when I close the bathroom door,
I swear it's been snowing in there for days.

Conception

I arrived between periods of a hockey
game, the product of a dishwasher
maybe, my father looking for a glass

and finding one in my mother's hand,
the warmth from a lifted plate
spreading across their faces, the reflection

above the sink reminding them they're alone
in the kitchen, and that snow, porcelain,
thick, gathers in drifts outside.

It's hard to believe they hadn't nodded
off, and that I should appear for
the first time vaguely like the onset of thirst,

the sweatered men in the basement skating
through static, holding their shapes
despite the distance they travelled.

And afterwards, the game going on,
one in front of the television, the other
lost in a book, the evening drawing

on and the snow still falling,
the street appearing from time to time
in the lights of a midnight plow.

Several Possible Explanations for the Appearance Then Disappearance of a South African Parakeet in Western Labrador

1

It was a stowaway,
a colourful hat worn through customs
by the daughter
of an immigrant mining family.

2

It flew out of a couch's pastel
patterns, a musty
living room spirit drawn to the wallpaper's vines.

3

It was perpetual: it poked
holes in the children's snowsuits.

It talked to shovels, the snow puddles
drying in the porch. It was curiosity
all covered with feathers:

summer trying to understand
the thermometer's fall.

4

It must have looked at winter
with the ambition
of a suntan salesman:

seeing its chance to make millions,
it flew out an open window,
flapping like an assembly of flags.

5

It was a collection of Salvation
Army handkerchiefs,
a hand glider in a hail storm,

a sea urchin arguing
with an assembly of waves.

6

It must have flown for blocks:
its lungs going asthmatic,
drying like wrinkled apricots

while the chambers of its heart
migrated to opposite poles.

7

It disappeared into us,
into the extended forecast,
the woods' imagination,
the streetlights' stationary tribe.

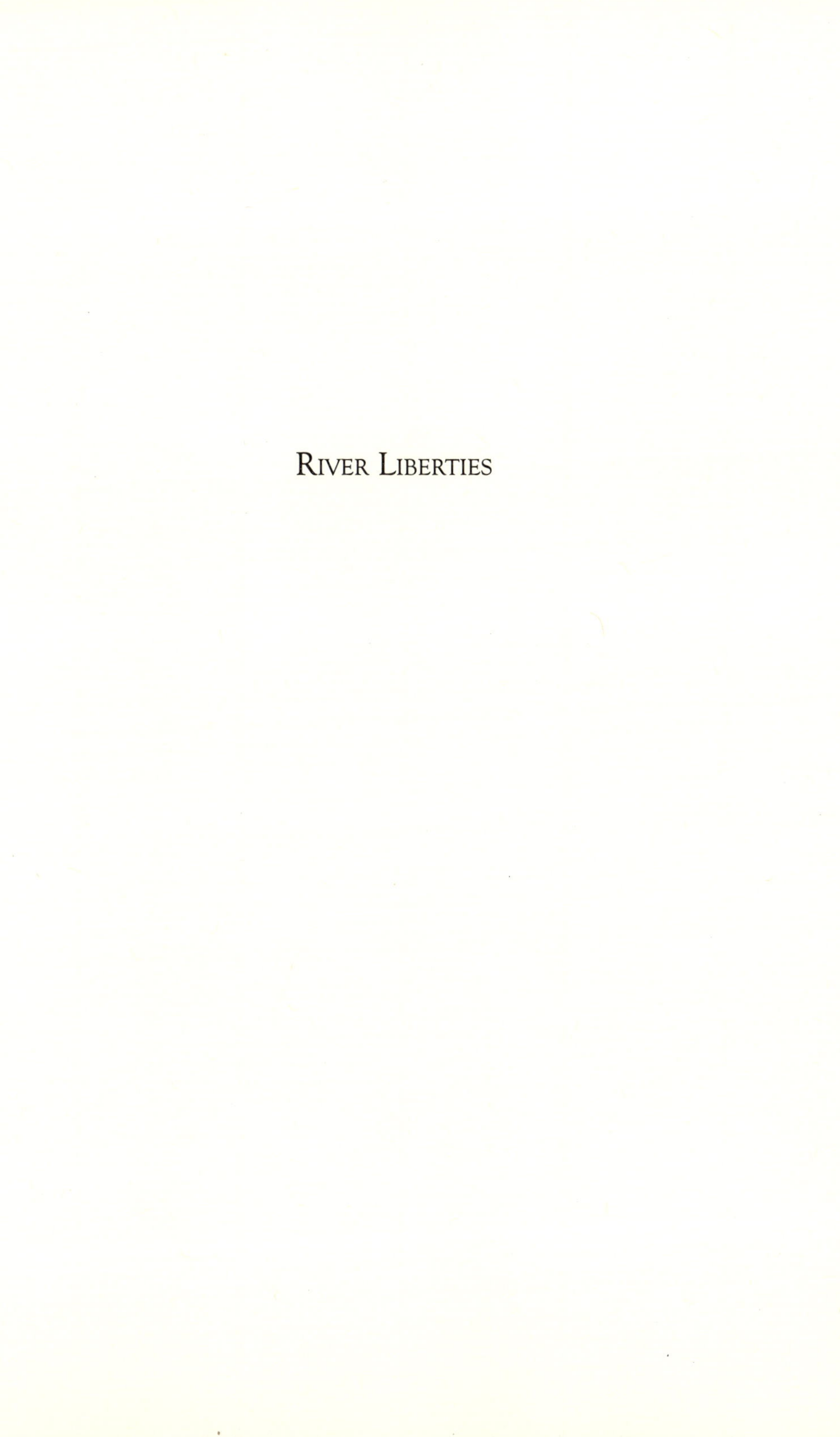

River Liberties

The more furious the star, the more brightly it burns.
This, my misreading of the cosmologist's
notebook: I saw the word furious, and took the midnight

sky for perforated anger. I thought, furious stars
look down at me nightly: furious with distance, furious
with equations of time and light, with symbols

still cross at the mathematicians who trapped them
in stone (under those Grecian skies). I thought
hydrogen compressing until it's pissed off,

hydrogen bursting into helium, a cold white
steam. (Thought, aimless walker, learn your thermal
dynamics before shooting them off at the mouth.)

Thought, no, it's actually the heaviest stars that burn
furiously: the weight of a star dictates its light.

Furiously, the weight of a star dictates its light.
How else would a mess of gas find its way
through the universe? How else would

such ideas come together, if not through sheer
violence, through the brute transformation
of one gas giving in on its own gravity.

What else but celestial betrayals to populate
the black above us, the darkness into which a city
empties when the world, relative to the sun,

holds itself upside down. And where else to begin
but with this river, still raw in December,
rain dulling its ice, the temperature breaking

up the continuous white, the warmth, like
a star's gravity, exposing the nerves of the city.

A star's gravity, exposing the nerves of the city,
pulling back the beech tree banks
so the river's frosted vertebrae show clear.

I ran that shoulder, along the water's dark
spine, and in March, skiing along the grey slate
of winter, have pushed with waxed edges,

thinking ski, skis, sky. Thought, I'm gliding
on a pair of skies. Where will that take me?
Once, in another forest, Bill Koch

invented skating, a technique that shifts
the body from side to side, turning us
to pendulum. And how simply it works:

by transferring our weight, by swaying,
a new geometry emerges from the snow.

A new geometry emerges from the snow,
misspelling my thoughts, likewise, into fresh
algebra. Into these scattered equations

let this river enter as an equals sign, balancing
me between its darkened banks, this walking
bridge a familiar probability. Onto this ice

let the footprints of a lost astronaut appear
in moonlight; let each print be mistaken
for a black and white satellite print of sky,

and let them be studied with the same diligence
as petrified stars. Let me travel, cold-
handed, across migrating sections of light,

the frozen reeds marking the place where
I became a passenger in my own listening.

I became a passenger in my own listening,
and noticed others travelling there too:
the red and white blink of a maintenance truck

on the Westmorland Bridge,
men and women in orange suits
quarantining lanes with sawhorses and

light. I noticed repairs slowing traffic
to a muffled chant, how city workers wave
their metal warnings, the contents of

their lungs wandering off like smoke from
an asphalt censer. And I noticed how,
by shovel or rake, they mend the turned-up stone:

with heat, with pressure, they thicken
the bridge, a tar altar for the river below.

The bridge, a tar altar for the river below,
follows the sun's absent
circumference to the city's north side.

Morning will find me crossing this
municipal arc, back pressed to
a slow bus, watching a star at the centre

of our system describe the river in
equatorial terms I'll not quite
configure. And this, the hardest part:

to stand here, knowing my hands will
not blow to the clarity of glass,
knowing it's simple flesh I'm stuck

with: this blood, that ache,
these tight-fisted, capillary thaws.

These tight-fisted capillary thaws,
this undressing river spectre revealing
its private debris: the torn sailboat

cartons, the broken glass assemblies,
the sunken tire and leaves. But
the water's movement is still endless

fume, still the black clerisy of winter
preserving itself as river bed, as
packed bend and turn: as sparrows

lifting overhead, their winged passports
open for the wind's approval
while the river wanders off, travelling

the night's eyeless socket,
pursuing a distant concern.

The Glass Desert

The Glass Desert

On July 16th, 1945, the first atomic bomb was detonated at the trinity site in New Mexico. The resulting fireball scorched the desert, heating the sand to glass. Samples from this area are extremely rare, since the site remains closed to the public. Each of our remnants was gathered by a team of specially-commissioned geologists, and comes with a certificate of authenticity. . . .

The glass desert is the desert compacted by heat.
At night, it's cool to the touch.

I spoke to an astronomer once who wanted to polish the glass desert.
He longed to gather its light.

Love, I would like a map of the glass desert for Christmas.
(If maps were made of glass, we could hold up our hometowns to
moonlight).

A tribe of window cleaners doing the breaststroke across the glass desert.
That's what I woke up to this morning.

An inspector came along one day and told the glass desert it was
no longer a desert. Look, I'm sorry, he said, but deserts are made of sand.
Not glass.

No one has ever crossed the glass desert.
Someday, I would like to try.

Listen, the inspector said, perhaps you'd be
happier as the desert's window.

After all, the desert's window is always open.
Every window longs to be a window to the desert.

But no one stares out the desert's window, replied the glass desert.
And the desert window is a poor place to hang plants.

Certainly, grandmothers do not cool
pies in the desert's window.

I like looking through this window,
but the view is not the same. Come back, fanciful

desert. You left your cactus in the doorway.
If I had to choose between a glass desert and the desert's window,

I would choose both. If a bowling ball rolled across the glass desert,
it would roll for a very long time.

The glass desert is the world's largest burn victim.
A tribe of midnight

travellers could circle it in less than two hours.
In less than two hours, I hope to have imagined a lifetime spent
staining its glass.

Acknowledgements:

Thanks to the editors of the following magazines who published some of these poems: *ARC*, *The Antigonish Review*, *Descant*, *Elysian Fields Quarterly*, *Event*, *The Fiddlehead*, *The Gaspereau Review*, *Grain*, *The Malahat Review*, *Maisonneuve*, *Pottersfield Portfolio*, and *Prism International*.

To the Prince Edward Island Arts Council, Arts New Brunswick, and the Canada Council for the Arts, thanks for support at various times.

My gratitude goes to my family, and to Kristina Bresnen. Thanks also to everyone who read this manuscript and who offered suggestions. In particular, thanks Richard Lemm, Ross Leckie, Dave Steeves, and John Mackenzie for helping shape this book. Finally, thanks to Eric Ormsby for his keen eye during the editorial stages, and to Dan Wells, for agreeing to publish this manuscript, and for seeing it through.

In the Lights of a Midnight Plow by David Hickey
was typeset in Goudy Old Style and Shannon Book,
and printed offset on Rolland Zephyr Laid
at Coach House Printing in an edition of 400 copies.

BIBLIOASIS
Windsor, Ontario